Also by Joel Allegretti

The Body in Equipoise

Europa/Nippon/New York: Poems/Not-Poems

Thrum

Father Silicon

The Plague Psalms

Edited by Joel Allegretti

Rabbit Ears: TV Poems

OUR DOLPHIN
A NOVELLA

Joel Allegretti

THRICE PUBLISHING

Thrice Publishing
PO Box 725114
Roselle, IL 60172
ThricePublishing.com

Our Dolphin
Copyright ©2016 by Joel Allegretti
JoelAllegretti.com
Book Design by David Simmer II and Thrice Arts
Author Photo by Jon Paul

First Thrice Publishing Edition: December 2016

ISBN-10: 1-945334-00-2
ISBN-13: 978-1-945334-00-9

Printed in the United States of America

ONE

In Emilio Canto's heat-infested dream, a gull of mythological proportions wrapped its claws around his slender body and bore him aloft. He stared down at the sea. The blue of the water soon gave way to the gray and green of the land. Emilio averted his eyes from the death that awaited him and looked at his hands. Instead of palms, fingers, and thumbs, two big crab claws protruded from his wrists. The wind ripped off his hood. There was a sharp pain in his belly, like a knifepoint poking him again and again. One of the awful bird's talons had punctured his flesh, but he didn't bleed.

"Wake up, Crab Face!"

The silhouettes of four young heads loomed above him, blocking the heavy Mediterranean sun. One boy pressed the sharp end of a stick into Emilio's stomach.

"Take off the hood. Show us the crab."

"Oh, leave him alone," another said. "He isn't bothering anybody."

A hand grabbed the top of his hood. Emilio held it fast.

"Why do we have to do this to him? Can't you see Emilio just wants to be left alone?"

The boy used his Christian name. Who was it? It was Serafino, who at sixteen, a year older than Emilio, swaggered like a ladies' man.

Emilio stood and brushed the sand off his legs. He curled his fingers into a tight ball, not to prepare himself for a brawl, but to keep from losing composure.

"I think Crab Face wants to fight."

Emilio tried to pass. A pudgy tan body blocked him.

"Going somewhere, Crab Face?"

"I want to go home," Emilio muttered.

"What was that?"

"I want to go home."

"I'll take you home," said Serafino.

Serafino's friends threw glances at each other.

"Are you going to hold his hand?"

He ignored the taunt. "Come on, Emilio."

They started walking away, and Emilio felt the sun against his naked face. To his horror, he saw the hood dangling between two fingers. The boy held it out to him.

"You forget this?"

The other boy snapped his arm back as soon as Emilio reached for the hood.

"Give it to me," Emilio pleaded. "Please give it to me."

"Come get it."

Three boys tossed the hood back and forth as a frantic Emilio darted from one to the other to retrieve it and held a hand in front of his face.

"You don't have to hide your mug from us. We know what you look like."

"Give it back to him," Serafino ordered.

Emilio scurried to and fro like a water bug trying to avoid a crushing foot. One of the boys waved the hood in Emilio's face like a flag. The boy was unaware of Serafino's fist until it landed square on his mouth. Blood dribbled down his chin. He dropped his prize. Serafino picked up the hood and handed it to Emilio, who pulled it over his head.

"Let's go, Emilio," Serafino said.

"You'll pay for this, Fino!" the bloodied boy threatened.

"I don't think I will."

Without looking back, Emilio walked ahead of Serafino. He kicked through the sand, unearthing tiny colored shells. As he and Serafino approached his house, a white curly-haired puppy scampered out to meet them. The dog barked at Serafino and sniffed at his feet. The smiling boy bent down to pick it up, but the dog sought shelter in its master's familiar arms. "What's its name?" Serafino asked.

"Lucia. I named her after my grandmother."

From the interior of the house, the voice of a tired woman called, "Emilio, is that you?"

"That's my mother."

Emilio stared at Serafino, envious of his face.

"If you want to come inside …" Emilio began.

"No," Serafino said. "I have to go home."

"Thanks, Serafino."

Serafino made an about-face and headed off, soon

becoming another part of the landscape.

"Emilio!" his mother called again. "Come in the house."

What she saw first were the stains on the hood. "Emilio, that's blood," she said, alarmed.

"I fell on the rocks and cut myself."

"Take off the hood and let me see it."

"I'm all right."

"Listen to me, Emilio Giovanni Canto."

"I'm not hurt."

"Why are you defying me? You're in the house now. You don't have to wear it."

Emilio removed the hood and tossed it on a chair. Giulietta inspected the face that brought her infinite despair. The right side was flawless, the skin soft and the color of a copper pot. The left side was half of a Carnival mask. The skin was hard and riddled with fissures, as if the boy had come out of the womb with a shell. This part of the jawbone, instead of curving under the chin, ended in serrated edges like a saw blade. The cheek and forehead hosted thorn-like protrusions. It was the doctor who, upon returning to his own house, said one side of the Canto baby's face resembled the back of a crab.

"I don't see any blood. Where did you fall?"

"I fell on the rocks."

"You know what I mean. Where did you hit your head?"

Giulietta knew by his failure to look her in the eye that he hadn't told the truth.

"Where did you hit your head?"

"There's a spider on the ceiling."

She looked to where he pointed. "I'll kill it in a minute.

Where did you hit your head?"

Giulietta could see his eyes tearing. Was it only her imagination, or did the eye on the monstrous side cry more than the other?

Emilio was supposed to have an older brother. The baby was born ready for a shroud. When Emilio came into the world, his parents decided they weren't meant to enjoy the pleasures of a large family. Leonardo's line would die with Emilio.

Emilio once overheard his parents discussing his lost brother. His mother said stillbirth was God's way of preventing a catastrophe. The child had no place in the world. When Emilio heard this, he wanted to know why the Lord allowed him to live. Dear Jesus, he thought, how could his brother have been more horrible to look upon than he?

TWO

The cry, rising and falling with the tide, reached Emilio's ears when the moon was high. It seeped into his sleep and clung to his dreams. Then it awakened him.

It sounded to Emilio like a goat's bleat, but the tone was almost human, the whimper of an injured child. Could Lucia have run out of the house and gotten trapped? No, she was lying on the floor asleep. Why hadn't she heard the cry? He threw off the bedclothes and tiptoed to the window, feeling his awkward way through the darkness.

He opened the shutters. Emilio rested his elbows on the sill and leaned out the window. He listened to the music of the sea. Floating above it was the cry.

"Did you hear that?" he asked Lucia, who was now awake and nosing at his bare calves. She looked at her master with admiring eyes and panted.

"It sounds like someone's been hurt."

His eyes scanned the coastline. They landed on a black shape, which Emilio thought was an upturned rowboat until he saw it move.

"There's something out there, Lucia. I think it's dying."

Naked and without his hood, Emilio hoisted himself through the window and lifted Lucia. Under the moon, the brown sands were gray, as if transformed into a plane of dust. Emilio paused about ten feet from the strange object. Lucia ran ahead. The dog circled it, retreated, and then growled.

It was a beached dolphin.

Emilio walked up to it. He crouched and stroked its snout. The dolphin was small, a calf that must have wandered away from its mother. Its cry was pitiful. Emilio would have sworn its eyes wept. He sat down and lifted the dolphin's head onto his lap.

"We have to get it back in the sea," Emilio told Lucia.

Emilio removed the head from his thigh and placed it on the sand. He ran back to the house and returned with a pail. He dunked it in the shallows and poured water over the dolphin. He repeated the gesture. He tossed the bucket aside, grasped the dolphin just above the tail fins, and tried to pull it backward into the sea. It wouldn't budge. Emilio positioned himself against the dolphin's back. Anchoring his feet in the sand and grinding his teeth until his jaws ached, he pushed. The dolphin shifted. Lucia snaked through Emilio's legs and licked his toes.

"Stop it," Emilio said.

He pushed harder. The dolphin's snout scraped against the sand. A pair of crabs waltzed at the water's edge.

Emilio's arms ached. The dolphin's cry subsided.

"We're almost there," he said.

The dolphin began to beat its pectoral fins when it sensed it was about to regain its place in the sea. The head was finally submerged. Seeing that success was within his reach, Emilio redoubled his effort. A splash of water struck Emilio's face when the dolphin returned to where it belonged. It then exploded out of the water and gyrated in the air as if it were performing a joyous dance at having found itself alive. Its black outline tore through the sheets of moonlight as it headed to the distant reaches of the Mediterranean Sea.

Emilio waded back to shore and sat his naked body on the sand.

"We did it," he said. "I can't wait to tell Papa. He'll be very proud of us."

The wind had a narcotic effect on them both. Emilio lay on his back and clasped his hands behind his head. Lucia curled up beside him.

Something troubled the water as it headed toward land. A pair of grateful eyes broke the surface and watched the sleeping youth.

"Thank you, Emilio," the dolphin said. "We'll see each other again very soon."

It spun like an acrobat and pursued the deep.

THREE

Giulietta's sister and her family came for dinner every Sunday after Mass. They, too, were victims of misfortune. Dona Granchio's first child, like Giulietta's first, was born dead. The second didn't live long enough to learn the meaning of a birthday. Dona at last gave birth to a boy who was healthy and unblemished. Federico was a year younger than Emilio and mortified at having a monster for a relative. If he spent any time with Emilio, it was at his mother's prodding.

"He's your only cousin," she told him. "You're both of the same blood."

"He's from the blood of the devil with that face."

Giulietta and Dona prepared the table as their husbands smoked and talked. The women laid out a platter of broiled fish, a tureen of bean soup, decanters of wine, bread, and pasta. Behind the house, Emilio and Federico played fetch with Lucia while they waited for their mothers to call them in for dinner.

"Emilio," Federico said in a low voice as he waved the stick in Lucia's face. He looked toward the house to make sure the adults weren't within listening distance.

"What?" Emilio asked.

"Guess what I did yesterday."

"What?"

"Aren't you going to try to guess?"

"I don't know."

"Come on, guess," an irritated Federico said.

Emilio just shrugged. "I can't guess."

Federico rolled his eyes. "All right, then I'll tell you." He reduced his voice to a whisper. "I touched a girl."

"Where?"

"What do you mean where? Where do you think, you moron?"

"What did it feel like?"

"Like the inside of a mussel. You know what else?"

"What?"

"She touched me."

"Really?"

"I let her play with it."

"Who was the girl?"

"I'm not telling. You ever touch a girl, Emilio?"

Emilio was silent.

"I didn't think so," Federico scoffed. "Hey, Emilio, where did those scratches come from?"

After Emilio recounted the details of his heroic night, Federico said, "You're lying."

"It's true," Emilio insisted. "You can ask Mama."

"Did she see you?"

"No, but I told her about it."

"She'll believe anything you say. She's going crazy from taking care of you."

Emilio's hands struck Federico's chest and sent him tumbling backwards. Federico sat up and rubbed his head, his eyes burning with anger.

"You made me do it," Emilio said.

"I'm going to tell Papa on you."

"I don't care. I'll do it again if you say anything else against Mama."

"I hate you."

"I still don't care."

Federico fired whatever insults came to mind. Emilio suffered them with a martyr's indulgence until Federico spoke those punishing words. It was the first time he heard a blood relative say the name to his face.

Emilio's fists drooped like wilted flowers. His arms fell to his sides. He had no desire to pretend Federico wasn't hurtful. He wasn't going to wear a mask of feigned passivity. One mask was more than enough.

"I'm glad it hurts," Federico said with a sneer. "I'll say it again: Crab Face!"

Emilio dashed away from his cousin, his house, his parents, his aunt and uncle, and the Sunday feast. He ran past people who called after him, asking what was wrong. Emilio didn't answer. He ran and ran. He headed for the water, running along the shoreline. He tore off the hood and was about to throw it into the sea. In a fragile moment of reasoning, he stuffed it into the front of his shorts. It didn't matter to him that his deformity was there for the neighbors to see. They knew how he looked, and they would say what they wanted to about him whether he wore the hood or not.

He raised his head and exposed his face to the sun in all its scorching majesty.

"Why don't you just burn it off?"

The sea's fragrances curled like smoke in his nostrils. He smelled brine and decayed fish and seaweed and pretended their aromas were those of the food he was missing. He wondered what was going on at his house. He pictured Federico fabricating some elaborate tale of how Emilio became angry for no reason and attacked him. He saw his father and uncle undertaking a search for him, while his mother cried at the table and her sister tried to comfort her. Federico would relax in the background, enjoying the chaos.

Growing restless, Emilio thought about going home, if for no other reason than his hunger. He continued on in his original direction.

Emilio arrived at a grotto. He climbed over rocks to peer inside. Emilio thought he would like to remain there for the rest of his life, where no one would think to look for him and where he wouldn't have to see or talk to anyone.

He sat on a rock, his vacant stare set on the sea and the sky. He was unaware that he himself was under surveillance, not from the grotto, not from a hidden spot in the brush, but from below him in the water.

•

"Marco, stop!" Giulietta pleaded with her brother-in-law. "He didn't mean it."

Marco slapped Federico until the boy's cheek looked sunburned. Federico tried to escape his father's volcanic fury, but the man's square-knot grip held him fast.

"I should tie a rope around your tongue and drag you behind the boat!" Marco roared.

Emilio was wrong. His cousin hadn't invented a report of unprovoked madness. When the adults asked him where Emilio had gone, Federico replied that he and his cousin had a fight and Emilio knocked him down.

"Then he ran off crying like a girl," Federico was quick to add.

•

Emilio decided to head home. He climbed down from the rock, scraping the backs of his legs. He withdrew the hood from his shorts, stared at the crumpled garment for a few seconds, and slipped it over his head. He looked with fondness at the grotto. "I'll be back tomorrow," he said.

"Emilio."

"What?" Did someone call him? There was a rustling in the trees. A bird took to the air.

Emilio started to walk away.

"Emilio."

He spun around. It was a boy's voice. Was it coming from inside the grotto?

"Who's there?"

His own echo answered him. Blue lizards with luminescent eyes peered over the rocks. He heard a splash. Someone was secluding himself.

Emilio backed away and was about to run with as much speed as his legs could generate, when the voice called out again.

"Don't run."

The water rippled and bubbled. Emilio's eyes brightened.

"Hello," he said to the dolphin. "I never thought I'd see you again."

He looked at the grotto again, waiting for the voice's owner to present himself.

"Don't look there, Emilio. Look at me."

"Where are you?"

"I'm right here."

Emilio was losing patience. How long would this eerie prank last? "Where is here?"

"Look in the water, right before your eyes."

"Is that you, Federico? If it is, I don't think it's funny."

"It's not Federico, whoever that is. It's me."

Emilio wanted to say something, but his voice failed him.

"Don't look at me like that, Emilio."

"You can't talk," Emilio said.

"I'm talking now."

"How?"

"The same way you do."

The dolphin's beak moved each time it spoke, but Emilio still couldn't believe what he saw. .

"Who's doing this?" he yelled into the air.

Then to the bushes, "Are you in there? Why are you doing this?"

"Emilio, look at me."

He faced the dolphin again.

"You're not talking to me," he said. "I don't believe it. There's someone around here playing a trick on me, and I won't fall for it."

"You're not convinced."

"I'm going home."

"Don't leave. I'll prove to you I'm talking."

Emilio folded his arms. "Prove it."

"Come into the water near me. Say anything you want. I'll repeat it exactly as you said it."

Emilio thought for a few moments and agreed to try. He waded in the water until he was only inches away from the dolphin.

"All right, Emilio. Say something. Say whatever you like."

"My name is Emilio Giovanni Canto," he said in a soft voice. "I'll be fifteen the day after tomorrow."

The dolphin recited the sentences word for word.

"I don't believe it," Emilio said.

"I told you."

Emilio petted the dolphin's head. The extraordinary animal chattered, once again becoming an ordinary citizen of the sea.

"Hang on," Emilio said. He withdrew his hand. "How do you know my name?"

"Didn't you just tell me your name was Emilio?"

"I mean before that. When I was sitting on the rock, you said, 'Emilio.' How did you know my name?"

"Do you know what I am?"

"You're a dolphin."

"How did you know that?"

Emilio thought back through his entire life. When did he learn the word? He couldn't remember.

"I don't know," he said. "I've always known what you are."

"And that's how I know who you are."

"Do you have a name?"

"Dolphin."

"I don't mean that. A dolphin is what you are, but it's

not your name. I'm a boy, like you're a dolphin, but my name's Emilio."

"Then I don't have a name. Why don't you give me one?"

"You want me to name you?"

"I'd like that very much," the dolphin said.

Emilio considered all the names he knew. Those of his parents and grandparents, the names of his neighbors, the names they gave their pets. He counted off the names of saints and the name of the parish priest. Finally, one name stood apart from all the others.

"I know what I'll call you," Emilio said.

"What's that?"

"Serafino."

"Serafino," the dolphin repeated. "What does it mean?"

"It's the name of someone I know."

"Is he a friend?"

"I hope so."

"I like it," the dolphin said.

"Then your name is Serafino," Emilio declared. "My parents won't believe what I have to tell them. I made friends with a dolphin that can talk."

"Wait, Emilio."

"What?"

"Your parents won't believe you if you tell them about me."

"When they see you..."

"They'll see me only for what I am."

"I don't understand."

"They won't hear me talk. No one will hear me talk except you."

"I still don't understand."

"You're the only one I have an interest in. So, you're the only one who'll hear me talk. Come into the water and hold onto me. I'll take you home."

Emilio gripped Serafino's dorsal fin with both hands. The dolphin plowed through the water. As he traveled, Emilio's eyes became prisms that changed his view of his lifelong surroundings. The world was now radiant. How he would like to tell his mother and father of the earth's hidden marvels. How he would like to tell everyone, but they would only laugh at him. "Crab Face has finally lost his mind. Well, I guess it was to be expected."

FOUR

Leonardo opened Emilio's door without knocking. The little room was dark, the shutters drawn. The boy was asleep. Leonardo walked in and stood beside the bed. He laid his hand on Emilio's shoulder. He pressed his fingertips into the facial barbs, which his calluses prevented him from feeling.

All men conceal from their wives some secret that shames them, be it a loss of desire or an infidelity. For this father, it happened right after Emilio was born. He wished at the foot of the infant's crib that compassionate angels would descend and take possession of Emilio's soul.

Leonardo walked to the window and cracked open a shutter. He saw the water's surface break apart.

"That dolphin is still there," he said to himself.

FIVE

Emilio sat on the edge of his bed with his legs crossed, staring out the window. Lucia snored on the floor, and no doubt his parents were doing the same in their bed. Emilio massaged his thighs.

Crickets chirped outside. He stepped over to the window to close the shutters. He hadn't seen Serafino in days. Maybe the dolphin was gone for good, off in quest of another like Emilio, someone else despised and shunned for whatever reason.

Emilio lifted his shorts and a shirt from the back of a chair. He pulled on his hood and left the house. He walked toward the center of town, through the narrow warrens of white houses. In the distance he saw the outlines of the mountains, the highest of them curved and full, like the breast of a nursing mother.

He headed to the church. Surprising to Emilio was that in the moonlight, the House of God didn't appear so welcoming. With shadows spilling like tar from its roof, it looked more like a haunted fortress than a sanctuary for the virtuous and wayward alike. He approached the front door. It wasn't locked. It never was. The church was dark, except for the tiny yellow candle flames that flickered like cats' eyes. Emilio dipped his fingers in the font of warm holy water and made the Sign of the Cross. He removed his hood. Since he was in the house of the One who gave him his face, there was no reason for him to hide it here.

Emilio gazed upon the face of the Madonna of the Bountiful Sea. Her statue rested on a pedestal to the right of the altar. Her marble eyes and chiseled lips bore the blessings of peace. Her hands, soft and loving even in stone, reached out as if to gather the entire world into the security of her embrace. O Queen of Heaven, mother of the Incomparable Child, you of the unblemished womb, can you tell us what this young man's reward will be?

Emilio found no comfort in the house where people sought it. He came with the burden of loneliness and would leave with it. His mother promised him that his was a righteous life, that the prize awaiting him in heaven was the envy of kings. Once upon a time, he accepted it, like everything she told him. Now, he no longer believed it. Emilio Giovanni Canto was nothing more than what others saw him as: a mistake of nature. He marched up the center aisle to the altar and scowled at the Crucifix. He knew he was treading on unsteady ground in the sanctified household, but didn't care. His breath, as if he were a bull, rushed in and out of his nostrils. Emilio stared at the bowed head of Christ and pointed an accusing forefinger at his own face.

"Tell me why you did this to me," he demanded of the figure.

"Look at me!" he shouted, then clapped his hand over his mouth. The force of his cry humbled him. Maybe the priest was in the sanctuary. Emilio fled the church.

IN PRAISE OF SERAFINO

The sea does not betray the ones it loves.

Beautiful and wondrous creature, how long have you traveled to undertake your labor of mercy?

How is it that you, peerless animal, became blessed? Do angels discuss you? Are you an agent of redemption, the patron saint of the outcast?

Why you, graceful sea beast? On whose command do you act? Do you know why you have the honor of such holy work? Can you teach others to be laudable? Who will be there to take your place when you leave this world?

Go, you miracle of the water. Encounter no impediment.

SIX

Emilio served Rodrigo his salted codfish and retired to the bow to eat his own dinner. He lost count of how many days they were at sea. Málaga would be the last port of call before they reached Tangier. Emilio meditated without end on the night he left his parents in secret, saying goodbye to them while they slept. With each momentous step he took away from his house, he heard the voice of his mind urging him to stay.

•

Emilio met Rodrigo at the dock. The Portuguese sailor was on his boat, lying in a hammock, emptying a bottle of Moscato, and rasping a filthy ditty about a woman in Hong Kong. He sneezed and sprayed a mouthful of wine all over his clothes.

"What the hell are you looking at?" Rodrigo demanded.

"I'm sorry," Emilio said. "I didn't mean to stare."

"And what's with that bag on your head? Are you hiding from someone or what?"

"I have to wear it."

"Why, for Christ's sake?"

"I don't have a nice face."

"Well, no one ever said I was anything to look twice at, but I never thought I had to hide my face from the world. Let me see that puss."

"No, I can't."

"Look, there isn't a thing you got wrong with you that can beat some of what I've seen in this world. Once I was in India and saw this guy who looked like a snake. I swear to God. He had no arms, and his legs were fused together like a tail. And his skin was all scale-like. So, your face can't look any worse than this guy. Come on, let me see it."

Emilio pulled off the hood. Rodrigo's eyebrows leaped up his forehead.

"Holy Mary, you weren't lying."

Emilio turned his face away from Rodrigo. Rather than recoiling, the sailor invited him aboard.

"Like I said, you aren't the worst I've seen. By the way, what are you doing down here so late? Shouldn't you be home in bed?"

"I'm running away."

"Oh, I see. What's the matter? Your Papa beat you too much?"

"No!" Emilio snapped. "My Papa's good to me."

A seagull cawed overhead. Emilio was getting sleepy. He yawned without covering his mouth.

"I'm kind of tired myself," Rodrigo said. "I'd offer you

a place, but all I got is this hammock, and it's where I sleep. Maybe you should be on your way, young fellow, because I got to be off very early. I got a long trip ahead of me."

"Where are you going?"

When Rodrigo said, "Tangier," Emilio became excited. "Take me with you."

"I don't know about that."

"Please," Emilio pleaded. "I'll work for you."

Rodrigo scratched his unshaven chin.

"Well, I could always use a hand."

"I promise I'll work hard for you."

Rodrigo chuckled and coughed up some phlegm, which he launched in an arc off the side of the boat. "I got no doubt about that, none at all."

•

One morning, Rodrigo sprained his ankle. He barked in agony as Emilio dislodged the shoe from the foot. Rodrigo brought his fist down on Emilio's head.

"Watch what you're doing, for Christ's sake."

The swollen foot bore the colors of the sky at sunset, all purple, blue, and scarlet.

Emilio thought of Serafino often. He watched the sea with longing, hoping the dolphin would appear. He imagined that Serafino, unaware of time's passing, was waiting for him at the grotto.

SEVEN

In a house owned by sorrow, she wandered again and again past a room that was unoccupied for too long. Sometimes she entered and sat on the bed, laying a hand on the pillow, hoping it would feel the warmth of a boy's head. Day after day, the pillow was cool. She would close her lusterless eyes and imagine he was there asleep or that he was down at the water. Something would nudge her hand or nestle in her lap, and she would open her eyes, thinking he was home safe and sound, only to see Lucia.

Her husband assured her the boy lost would soon be the boy found. What he didn't tell her, and vowed he never would, was that every morning he scoured the beach for their son's remains.

EIGHT

The North African sun was a luminous gold when they reached the port of Tangier. Men sheathed in white tunics, their faces the color of rosewood, wandered about the dock. Emilio spied a group of musicians sitting cross-legged on a rug playing instruments he had never seen. Every so often, a man who picked an ornate lute broke into a disturbing wail, like that of a forgotten soul crying for the attention of God or a lover. Emilio noticed men kneeling on mats, touching their foreheads to the ground. He asked Rodrigo what they were doing.

"They're praying to Allah," the sailor explained.

"Who's Allah?"

"Allah is the God of the Muslims."

"What are Muslims?"

Rodrigo scowled. "You don't know a hell of a lot,

do you? Muslims are people who believe a man called Muhammad delivered God's word."

"Are there many Muslims?"

"There are millions."

This fascinated Emilio. If he ever returned home, he would have marvelous tales to tell. He knew no faith other than his parents' Roman Catholicism. He had heard of the Jews, but he knew only what the villagers told him, that they were a devious people whose forebears murdered the Son of God. An old woman once told his mother that his face was the fruit of a Jew's sorcery. How this could be, since there were no Jews in his village, went unexplained.

The men on the mats chanted things he didn't understand.

"What language are those men singing in?" he asked.

"Arabic."

"Do you understand it?"

"Better than I speak it. It doesn't make any difference. People speak many languages here. The world comes to Tangier. You'll meet people who not only speak your language, but three or four others, as well. But I'm warning you, you have to be careful who you deal with here. You'll find people who'll say one thing and mean the other. Stay close and don't get lost. Tangier invites you to get into serious trouble."

Several of the Moroccan men pointed at Emilio and laughed. He realized then that his face was bare. He put on his hood.

"That's probably a good idea, though either way you'll get looks. Let's get off this boat."

"Where are we going?"

"First, we'll get a bite to eat. Then we'll go to a hotel."

The word "hotel" fell upon Emilio's ears like a prayer. He envisioned a comfortable bed with clean, cool sheets and a bathtub.

Emilio helped Rodrigo down from the boat. Rodrigo walked with the aid of a cane made from a broomstick. A locust plague of men overwhelmed them, shoving all sorts of articles under their noses: brass plates, fabrics, and leather valises that stank like ripe cheese. Rodrigo waved away the belligerent vendors. One seller yelled inches away from Rodrigo's face in Maghrebi. Rodrigo pulled his head back with annoyance and replied in his own language. The Moroccan switched to Portuguese. Rodrigo then spoke a couple of sentences in Spanish. The vendor responded in kind. Rodrigo shifted to Greek, and the native proved capable in that tongue, as well. It astounded Emilio to hear these men vault from one language to another. A man with spidery fingers shoved a mirror against his chest, promising him an incomparable bargain. Emilio pushed the mirror away and begged Rodrigo to deliver him from all this madness.

"This is Tangier," Rodrigo said. "Get used to it."

They made their way through the high walls of the medina, a chaotic market of lamb carcasses, mounds of olives that glistened like black and green pearls, and hills of teas. They passed successions of veiled women and men leaning against doorways. Everywhere there was music, which didn't seem to emanate from any one place. It descended from the sky like drizzle. It seeped through the ground and vibrated in their feet. The music had neither beginning nor end. It just was.

Rodrigo ignored the merchants who called for him

to inspect their wares as he hobbled by their stalls. Whenever Emilio wanted to stop to examine something that interested him, Rodrigo said, " Keep walking."

Emilio noticed a policeman watching them. Each time he looked back, the officer was following at a measured distance.

"There's a policeman," he said. "Does he think we're guilty of something?"

"Everybody in this city is guilty of something," Rodrigo said.

They stopped at a café. The waiter took them through a back door into a courtyard that umbrellas shielded from the sun. They occupied a table near two men who played cards and shared a water pipe.

Rodrigo lifted his injured foot and rested it on a low stool.

"You should see a doctor about your foot," Emilio suggested.

"The only way doctors here will treat a foot is by cutting it off. It'll heal on its own."

"You're in pain."

"I won't be for long."

A burning scent streamed into Emilio's nostrils, heady incense that made the sides of his skull hum. He saw that it originated in the smoke from the card players' pipe. A shabby waiter set down two glasses of hot mint tea. Emilio reached for his glass, which scalded his fingers. The waiter showed him how to hold it. He then spoke to Rodrigo in French. Rodrigo nodded and replied. Emilio guessed they were talking about him, since the waiter every so often looked in his direction. Rodrigo then said three short words in French. The waiter bowed and retreated into the café.

"What were you talking about?" Emilio asked.

"You."

"What did he say?"

"He wanted to know why you're wearing that hood, so I told him."

"Rodrigo, how many languages do you speak?"

"As many as I need to."

"I wish I could speak different languages. I'd like to be able to speak to anyone anyplace in the world."

Emilio again thought of Serafino. If the dolphin was able to communicate with him in Italian, then couldn't it carry on a conversation with other people in their language? And if the dolphin had the power of speech, would it not be possible for other animals to have the same ability? Emilio envisioned a miraculous world in which goats sang hymns, parrots delivered sermons from the pulpit, and pigs offered eulogies at funerals.

"Rodrigo, can you talk to anyone in his language?"

The sailor gave him a lazy smirk.

"Drink your tea."

Emilio didn't like the tea. He set the glass back on the table, and two huge green flies rendezvoused around the rim. Rodrigo slurped his tea and wiped his mouth on the back of his hand.

"I'll drink yours if you don't want it," the sailor said.

Emilio heard his stomach rumble. So did Rodrigo.

"Is that drumbeat coming from you, Emilio?"

"I'm very hungry."

"Sit tight. Lunch is on the way."

The waiter brought a large platter. He placed it in the center of the table and lifted the lid to reveal a pyramid of cooked grain topped with chicken, carrots, potatoes, green peppers, and chickpeas. The rising steam was fragrant with spices. There was enough food for four.

"Let's eat," Rodrigo said.

Rodrigo plunged into the food, ravaging it with both hands. Emilio joined him. When they finished, Rodrigo sat back and belched with satisfaction. The card players, still involved in their game, looked at him and shook their heads.

"You have enough?" Rodrigo asked.

Emilio nodded. Rodrigo picked a lemon wedge from the platter. He squeezed it between his teeth, sucked the juice from the pulp, and gnawed on the bitter rind. The waiter came by to clear the plates and returned with more tea and a small dish of sticky brown confections. Rodrigo took one, bit into it, and savored the flavor. He pushed the dish toward Emilio.

"Have one."

Emilio brought the dessert to his nose.

"You're supposed to eat it, not sniff it like a dog."

"What is it?"

"It's called majoun."

"What's in it?"

"All kinds of good things," Rodrigo said, "Dates, honey, chopped nuts, and a little special something."

"What's the special something?"

"The same thing they're smoking," Rodrigo said, casting his eyes toward the card players. Sometimes one would say something, and many moments would pass before the other replied.

"Go ahead, Emilio, try one."

Emilio nibbled like a squirrel. The majoun was sweet,

and he enjoyed the taste of the dried fruit and anonymous spices. He ate another.

"You like it?" Rodrigo asked. He watched the boy with glee. "Have as many as you want. Eat the whole plate if you like."

The waiter materialized at Rodrigo's side and handed him a quartered slip of paper. Rodrigo unfolded the paper, read the address the waiter had written on it, and stuffed it in his breast pocket. He thanked the waiter, who bowed, coughed into his sleeve, and disappeared once more into the café.

Emilio devoured four of the majoun balls. His cheeks were hot. His fingers and temples tingled with the electric charge of jellyfish stings. Worse than these sensations was the nausea that smoldered in the pit of his stomach. He pressed his hand against his belly.

"Rodrigo," he croaked. "I'm sick. I think I'm dying."

The Portuguese's laugh roared against his eardrums.

"You're not dying, Emilio. You'll be fine."

"Why do I feel so bad?"

"You ate that majoun like you were afraid a hawk was going to swoop down and snatch it."

The waiter tapped Rodrigo on the shoulder.

"Will there be anything else, sir?"

"No, thank you. That'll be it."

Rodrigo paid the man. "Thanks for your help," he said with a wink. The waiter grinned, exposing two rows of crooked teeth.

"It was my pleasure, sir."

Emilio laid his palms flat on the table for support and made a futile attempt to stand. He fell against Rodrigo, who helped him back to his seat.

"Easy there," Rodrigo said. "I don't need a broken leg, too."

A thick pressure bore into Emilio's armpits that seemed to want to lift him high. It was only Rodrigo bringing him to his feet. Emilio's knees buckled. Rodrigo wound his muscular arm around the boy like a python around a rodent.

They left the café and trudged through the market-place like maimed beggars. Rodrigo led Emilio along, the boy moving with him in fits and starts. Emilio had no faith in his vision, perceiving neither distance nor nearness. A street vendor hawking his merchandise a hundred yards away may just as well have been dangling from Emilio's eyelashes. The flies around his head could have been tracing circles around the sun.

Rodrigo propped Emilio up against a wall. Sweat ran like tears down the sailor's cheeks. He poked his fingers into his shirt pocket to retrieve the paper the waiter had given him. He read the address and searched up and down the street for a clue that would help him figure out where it might be. A buzzing tickled his ear. What he took to be the drone of a bee was Emilio humming.

"I'm starting to think you're causing more trouble than you're worth," he told Emilio, who didn't hear him.

Emilio slumped to the ground. A stray dog with scabs on its paws crept out from the shadows and sniffed at his hidden face. Rodrigo swung the broomstick down on the animal's haunches. The dog ran yelping down the street. With great discomfort, Rodrigo bent over and hoisted Emilio from the ground. He sat the boy up with his back to the wall.

"Knock it off, will you," Rodrigo said. "Everybody

will think I did you in. You can't hold your kif, that's your problem."

Rodrigo stopped a bearded man in sunglasses and European clothes.

"Excuse me," Rodrigo said in faulty Arabic. "I need help finding an address."

The passerby turned to him, and Rodrigo sensed he didn't approve of the sailor's look.

"Yes?" the man said.

"I'm trying to find an address."

The man sighed. "Would you feel more comfortable if we didn't speak Arabic? Do you speak French?"

"Yes."

"Then we've found some common ground. How may I help you?"

Rodrigo handed him the crumpled paper.

"Do you know where this address is?"

The man read the writing and then peered at Rodrigo over the top of his sunglasses. He cast a glance at Emilio, who seemed unaware of the man's presence. He handed the paper back to Rodrigo.

"What's the matter with the boy?"

"He's sick," Rodrigo said. "Something he ate."

"I wasn't referring to that," the man said. "I meant his rather unusual headgear."

"Oh, that. He's got a messed-up face."

"Indeed."

"Indeed. Now, about that address."

"Yes, I know where it is." He gave Rodrigo directions. Rodrigo thanked him. The man bowed and proceeded up the street.

Rodrigo reached down to take Emilio by the arm

and tried to avoid putting too much weight on his ankle. "Let's go, Emilio. Come on, get up."

"Can't I stay here and sleep?" Emilio mumbled.

"Don't worry. There'll be plenty of time for sleep. We're almost there."

"Where?"

"A place to sleep. Now, get up."

"I'm sick."

"No, you're not. You just think you are."

Emilio managed to stand and would have fallen again had he not been holding onto Rodrigo, who himself was having trouble staying erect.

"You sure aren't making this easy for me," Rodrigo said.

They shambled along, Rodrigo supported by the broomstick and Emilio kept on his feet by Rodrigo. The vendors' cries and the muezzin's call to prayer clashed like cymbals in Emilio's ears.

"I want to sleep," he said again.

"You'll get your chance."

They rounded a corner and stole into a shadowed alley. Ahead of them was a wrought-iron gate and beyond that, a triangle of light. They moved toward the light and soon were in the middle of a courtyard. The air smelled of roasting lamb and damp laundry. Somewhere above them, in the geometric ascension of balconies and apartments, a male voice shouted. Children's laughter trilled out of open windows.

Rodrigo stopped to look around. He shook his head in disgust. "I don't know where the hell this place is," he said to no one.

Emilio was almost fast asleep on Rodrigo's shoulder.

Rodrigo leaned on his broomstick. "You better be worth my while."

"What?" the dazed boy asked.

"I didn't say a thing."

Rodrigo spied a stone bench in the shade between two blighted lemon trees. Holding Emilio around the waist, he stumbled to the bench and sat the boy down. Before Rodrigo could take a seat, Emilio was lying face down with his arms hanging to the ground.

Rodrigo rested his back against one of the trees. The citrus scent tickled his nostrils. He was thirsty. He looked down at Emilio, who snored and moaned. He then leaned his head back and closed his eyes. He, too, was on the cusp of sleep when something hard bounced off his leg. Startled, he shook his head and opened his eyes. A ball rolled away from him. Two children, a boy and a girl, both around ten years old, ran to retrieve it and stopped when they saw Rodrigo.

"Watch where you're playing," he said in Portuguese.

The children stared at him, uncomprehending. He repeated the order in French. The boy picked up the ball and started to run, with the girl in tow.

"Wait a second," Rodrigo shouted in French. "I want to ask you something."

They didn't heed him and were about to vanish into the shadows.

"I'll give you money," he added in Maghrebi.

They stopped and turned around.

I knew that would get them, he thought.

"Money!"

The boy stood like a haughty prince with the ball under one arm. The girl hid behind him, peeking over his shoulder.

"Let me see it," the boy said in Maghrebi.

"I'm not so good with the local tongue," Rodrigo said. "Why don't we speak French?"

"Because I hate French," the boy said, again in Maghrebi.

"Jesus!" Rodrigo muttered. He dug his hands into his pockets and withdrew a few coins.

"Here," he said. "If you help me, you get money."

The girl whispered something to the boy. He told her to be quiet. He handed her the ball and strode up to Rodrigo. The sailor held the money in the extended palm of one hand and the slip of paper between two fingers of the other.

"All I want to know," Rodrigo said, "is if you can tell me where this address is." He said in French what he couldn't manage in Maghrebi.

The boy snatched the paper and scanned the writing. He stared at it for what seemed a long time.

"Well?" Rodrigo asked.

The boy returned the paper. He gave Rodrigo a vacant, silent look.

"God almighty, say something," Rodrigo demanded.

"I can't read," the boy said and, quick as a gnat, was gone with Rodrigo's money. He and his companion skipped into a doorway, squealing like the children they were. Rodrigo tore the paper into confetti. He saw the children's faces peeking out from the darkness. He shook his fist.

"Pray I don't get a hold of you or I'll rip your spines out with my bare hands!" he screamed in Portuguese.

Rodrigo scraped some rheum from the corner of

his eye and flicked it in their direction. He had another thought.

"What the hell do I have to lose?"

He called the address out to the children.

"Do you know where it is?" he shouted in French and added in Maghrebi, "I gave you money."

He saw the boy's finger point toward another iron gate. "It's through there."

"And then what?"

"It's through there," the boy repeated and disappeared into the interior of the house.

Rodrigo still heard their laughter, which grew fainter until it faded out altogether. His eyes wandered to the gate.

"Through there. This is taking forever."

He prodded Emilio with the broomstick. Emilio groaned.

"Up you go."

It took some time to rouse Emilio. They passed through the gate into a second courtyard identical to the one they had just left, with the same odors of meat and wash. Emilio began to sing a fisherman's work song and within short order found his voice held captive in his throat when Rodrigo pressed his hand over Emilio's mouth.

"Shut the hell up!"

At the far end of the courtyard was a blue and yellow door, which led into a building that looked like a private home.

"Emilio, I think we found the place," Rodrigo said with hope.

A brass knocker in the image of a cherub hung from

the door. Rodrigo banged it hard against the metal plate. The door opened, and he confronted an obese man almost six feet tall with thinning blond hair, a powdered face, and a cyst over his left eye. The man appeared to be an aristocrat of some sort, attired in white linen slacks and a Japanese silk dressing gown. His teeth clenched an ivory cigarette holder. With his heavy perfume, he smelled like a dowager. His green eyes bulged at the sight of the miserable visitors.

"How can I help you?" he asked in English. He spoke with a British accent.

Rodrigo didn't speak English, though he recognized the sound of it. "French?" he asked.

"Yes, indeed," the Englishman said. "Now, what can I do for you?"

"I got someone for you."

The man removed his cigarette holder and licked his lips.

"Is he drugged?"

"Majoun," Rodrigo answered.

"Quite right, quite right. Is there a particular reason for the hood?"

"I'll show you, but not out here."

"Very well," the fat man said. "Come in."

NINE

"Your name is Serafino?"

"Yes, Mother."

"Do you know why he gave you the name?"

"He told me I was named for someone special."

"It's a good name. Do you like it?"

"I do, Mother," Serafino said.

"Emilio has run away from home."

"He has?"

"Yes, and he's in terrible trouble. Bring him back."

"I don't know where he is," Serafino said in a panic.

"I do, and I'll tell you how to get there."

She gave him explicit instructions, but didn't describe Emilio's peril, because the dolphin wouldn't have understood.

"You know he's your responsibility, don't you?"

"Yes, Mother."

"Then please, go find Emilio."

"I will, Mother."

The dolphin was off with the collective speed of a hundred of his kind, through tides both furious and calm. After many leagues, he looked back and in the distance still could see her, who was incapable of leading him astray.

TEN

When he regained his senses, Emilio found himself face down on a bed, wearing a pair of beige cotton trousers. He was shirtless. A table at the center of the room held a silver serving tray with a teapot and glasses. The lavender walls were home to cheap Victorian-style landscapes. The shutters of the one window were wide open.

Emilio hopped off the bed, walked over to the window, and gazed out at a maze of rooftops. He heard below him the clamor of daily life in the medina. Beyond was the harbor, as blue as the sky. He looked toward the far reaches of the sea. Somewhere on the other side was the familiar world he cast aside.

"Where is Rodrigo?" was the first question he asked himself, not "Where am I?" He tried the door. Someone had locked it from the outside. Emilio returned to the window to determine the distance to the street. He would never be able to make it unbroken.

The door opened on creaking hinges. Emilio spun around and confronted a boy as slender and brown as himself. At first, Emilio thought he was looking in a mirror, because the boy wore a hood much like his. The youth entered carrying a large dish, his hands concealed in white gloves. Without a greeting of any kind, he slid it halfway across the table. He removed the tray that held the teapot and glasses.

"It's for you," he said. "Eat."

Emilio didn't expect to hear himself spoken to in Italian. The boy was through the door when Emilio called him back.

"You know Italian?"

The boy nodded.

"Why are you wearing that hood?" Emilio asked. It wasn't lost on him that this was his first opportunity to ask the question of someone else.

"Leprosy," the other boy replied. He laid the tea service on a chair

"Well, aren't you going to ask me why I'm wearing one?" Emilio asked.

"I already know why. I saw it. What happened to you?"

"I was born like this."

Emilio guessed the youth was around his age, but the boy had the world-weary manner of an old man.

"What's your name?" Emilio asked.

"Hassan."

"I'm Emilio."

"Hello."

A request lodged in Emilio's throat like a fish bone, one he knew too well and despised. Nonetheless, he himself had to submit it.

"Will you show me your face?"

Emilio believed that since Hassan had seen his face, he had a right to a glimpse of Hassan's. Unlike Emilio, Hassan didn't raise his voice in protest. He accepted the appeal as if Emilio was asking for a spoonful of pepper to season his food.

Hassan took off his hood. The revelation of the corroded face filled Emilio with neither revulsion nor empathy. Instead, his heart flew high on mirthful wings. Here before him was another who had to bear the curse of a face nobody wanted to see.

Hassan didn't stop with the hood. He took off his gloves to reveal fingers that could no longer be known as fingers. Emilio opened his hand and looked at his own, which were long and fine. His mother told him he had a musician's fingers, whatever that meant.

Emilio decided he had no reason at the moment to keep disguised. He freed his face. He then examined the plate of food.

"Why don't you have something to eat with me?"

"Thank you. I'm not hungry."

"Why don't you sit with me while I eat?"

Hassan looked to the door and after some deliberation said he would stay. Emilio expected the boy to join him at the table. Hassan instead sprawled out on the bed on his stomach, resting his head on crossed arms. Emilio sat so he could face Hassan. He popped an olive in his mouth and rolled it around as his teeth scraped the salty flesh from the pit, which he spat onto his plate. He felt uncomfortable eating in front of Hassan and again invited him to share his food. Hassan shook his head. Emilio, famished, devoured the overcooked lamb chops and fried potatoes.

After chewing the gristle off a bone, Emilio pushed the empty plate away and drank a glass of mineral water. The bubbles tickled his throat. From the street, the cloud-soft melody of a flute wound up to his window, along with the din of street vendors. Emilio couldn't believe there was so much cacophony in one place. Outside his window at home, everything spoke in whispers.

"How can you live with all this noise?"

"I don't hear anything," Hassan sighed.

Emilio eased over to the window and closed the shutters, denying entrance not only to sound, but also light. He took a seat on a sofa.

"Where's Rodrigo?" Emilio asked.

"Who's Rodrigo?"

"The man I was with."

"You mean the one with the bad foot? He's gone."

"Where did he go?"

"Who knows?" Hassan said. "Mr. Charles paid him for you, and then he left. Mr. Charles thinks you cost too much money."

Emilio stared at Hassan, not grasping what the leper was telling him.

"He got paid for me? You mean Rodrigo sold me? Answer me."

"Mr. Charles bought you, and he'll sell you, over and over."

"Who's Mr. Charles?"

"He's the man who runs the house. He came from

England. He's been here for years."

"What is this place? Isn't it a hotel?"

"In a way, but nobody stays more than a night."

Hassan described Emilio's new lodgings. When Emilio learned what purpose he would serve, he crossed himself. He couldn't understand why any man would want somebody who looked like him.

"We get men with every kind of taste," Hassan said.

And did Hassan allow himself to be put to use this way?

"My disease makes it impossible for anybody to want me, praise be to the merciful and compassionate Allah."

Why was he here then?

"I do things around the house for Mr. Charles. He feeds me and gives me a bed. My family gets money."

Besides Mr. Charles, Hassan continued telling the new captive, there was one other adult resident, an American named Moore, who rented a room. There were rumors he killed a member of his family, which was the reason he came to Tangier.

Hassan asked Emilio about his home. Emilio painted a vivid picture. He spoke of his father's house and his mother's sweetness. He imitated Lucia's bark when she wanted to play. He even told Hassan about the dolphin, though not about Serafino's magical ability.

"Your home sounds beautiful. Why did you want to leave?"

Emilio indicated his face.

"Ah, so your mother and father couldn't bear to look at you."

"Not them. It was everyone else."

"Ah," Hassan repeated.

"Why the devil is it so dark in here?" a haughty voice demanded from the doorway. "Let's say we get some light in this room, shall we?"

A broad figure approached the window with a delicate step, which was at odds with his size, and threw open the shutters.

"There, that's so much better," he said in English with affected satisfaction. He turned to Emilio and Hassan. He grinned and dabbed his perspiring forehead with a handkerchief.

"I see by the looks of things that my two exquisite freaks have become acquainted." He spoke flawless Italian. "Am I right, Hassan?"

"Yes, Mr. Charles."

"You're Mr. Charles?" Emilio inquired.

The man slipped his hands into the pockets of his dressing gown.

"I see you know who I am. Hassan, you naughty, naughty imp, what have you been telling our new friend about me? I'm sure you told him the most vicious tales."

Hassan squirmed on the bed and tried to avoid Mr. Charles's eyes.

"I didn't tell him anything, Mr. Charles," Hassan said.

Mr. Charles turned back to Emilio and said, "I'm sure he's lying through his teeth. That's the way it is with the natives in this godforsaken city. They're natural-born liars, every last one of them. Nevertheless, our Hassan here is a decent enough boy. He can't help being the way he is. It's inbred."

Mr. Charles sat next to Hassan. He fumbled in his pockets and withdrew a pair of white theater gloves, slipping them on with florid hand gestures. He winked at

Emilio then closed his fingers around Hassan's neck.

"Of course you wouldn't say anything untrue about your guardian now, would you?"

"No, sir," Hassan gasped as the fingers clutched tighter.

"Of course, you wouldn't. Not after I picked you out of the gutter and gave you a place to stay. Not when I keep your family fed. Am I right, Hassan, you despicable urchin?"

"Yes, sir," Hassan said.

Mr. Charles was speaking to Hassan in Maghrebi, which left Emilio at a loss. Emilio wanted to do or say something to help Hassan, but was too frightened to move.

Mr. Charles released his grip and pulled off his gloves. Hassan rubbed his neck with the stumps that once had been his fingers. Mr. Charles rolled his eyes.

"Good Lord, why do you waste your time?" he said in Italian. "You barely have a hand left. God only knows why I keep you here. I'm too compassionate for my own good. That's my problem. O Ellsworth Charles, when will you learn to think about yourself for a change?"

Mr. Charles stuffed the gloves in his pocket and stood. He glared at Emilio and puckered his lips.

"Yes, I know," Mr. Charles said. "You're wondering why I put on gloves. Our Hassan isn't contagious. Still, one never can be too careful, can one?"

Continuing in Emilio's language, he said, "Hassan, would you please—and do take note of the fact that I am saying please—would you please put yourself together, meaning hide your face and hands, and leave us. I want to get acquainted with our utterly fascinating guest."

Emilio's eyes pleaded with Hassan not to leave, but Hassan was out of the room within seconds. Mr. Charles looked at the closed door from the corners of his eyes.

"I will never understand for the rest of my life why I let that piece of street garbage stay here," he reiterated. "It's not as if he can contribute anything of value to this establishment."

He sauntered over to the sofa. He smiled and bared his teeth, one of which gleamed with a pinhead of red light: a ruby chip. As he came closer, Emilio noticed Mr. Charles was wearing mascara. Emilio retreated further into the corner of the sofa.

"Now," Mr. Charles began, "let me take a good look at you. Let me see what I spent my hard-earned money on. I know I paid considerably more than you're worth. It was the only way I could get rid of the detestable brute that escorted you here. My God, if you gave that man a bar of soap, I swear he wouldn't know what it was for. He'd probably try to eat it. You didn't exactly sparkle, either. It took the better part of an hour to clean you up."

Emilio viewed Mr. Charles not with alarm now, but hatred.

"Why are you looking at me like that?" Mr. Charles asked. "I'm getting the distinct impression you don't care for me. I certainly hope that's not the case. You see, I'm a very sensitive person. I can't bear it when someone doesn't like me. Since you're going to be staying with us—and I do mean staying—I want us to become the very best of friends. Now, you already know my name. Why don't you tell me yours?"

Emilio didn't answer. Mr. Charles raised his chin and pressed his doughy fists against his hips. A slipper-clad foot tapped the floor.

"My goodness, we're not being very cooperative, are we? I do not like repeating myself." Almost snarling, Mr. Charles asked through clenched teeth, "What is your name?"

Emilio remembered what just happened to Hassan.

"Well?"

"Emilio Giovanni Canto."

"That's better. I knew you'd see the error of your ways. Tell me, Emilio Giovanni Canto, where are you from? What is the paradise Emilio Giovanni Canto calls home?"

Emilio told him.

"I can't say I've heard of the place. I personally never saw the need to travel beyond Rome and Venice. Have you been to either? Of course, you haven't. Is your fragment of heaven anywhere near Rome or Venice?"

Emilio shook his head.

Mr. Charles dipped his fingers into his pocket and withdrew his cigarette holder. From another pocket he pulled out a small silver case. He opened it and removed a hand-rolled cigarette, which he twisted into the end of the holder. He lit the cigarette, drew hard on the mouthpiece, and held the smoke in his lungs for some moments before expelling it. Mr. Charles offered Emilio the cigarette holder.

"Would you like some kif?"

"No."

"Are you sure? It will put you in a delicious frame of mind."

"No."

"Suit yourself."

Mr. Charles dragged again on the cigarette holder and blew the smoke out through his nose. His hand lighted on the boy's thigh.

"Good God, there's barely an ounce of meat on your bones."

Emilio gagged on the smoke.

"I see you're having trouble breathing," Mr. Charles said. "I'll save it for later."

He caressed Emilio's thigh. Emilio drew his leg up. Mr. Charles giggled and laid the cigarette holder across an ashtray. He leaned in toward Emilio.

"Now, let's take a good look at you," Mr. Charles said. "My, my, my, that is an unusual birth defect. I don't believe I've ever seen anything quite like it before. And in Tangier you see quite a lot. Most of our clients prefer boys who are pretty. I'm hazarding a guess that you have some novelty value. There are those rare types who would pay a handsome price for something different. And you, Emilio Giovanni Canto, are something different. Maybe I should try you out first."

Mr. Charles traced a manicured fingertip up and down Emilio's bare chest. Emilio swallowed hard. "So smooth, so brown," Mr. Charles cooed.

Emilio's eyes settled on the ashtray. Emilio hesitated. His throat was dry, and the blood bubbled in his veins. He grabbed the cigarette holder and plunged the hot end into Mr. Charles's left eye. Emilio leaped from the sofa and headed for the door, his hood in hand.

The howl that burst from Mr. Charles's throat rattled the walls of the entire house. "I'll kill you!" he screeched. "Somebody help me! Damn it, help me!"

Emilio raced through the corridor, pushing aside

young boys and old men. Mr. Charles appeared in the hallway, holding a palm over his eye.

"Don't stand there gawking at me!" he bellowed. "Drag the vile thing back here!"

By that time, though, Emilio belonged to Tangier's spice-scented streets.

ELEVEN

The kindhearted dolphin plied the waves, stopping neither to eat nor to rest, swimming toward a realm of minarets and marketplaces.

TWELVE

In the glass shop's storage area, where he slept, Emilio lay on a tassel carpet listening to the rain. This was his fourth night in the shop.

•

The proprietor, an elderly Moroccan, found him roving the medina hungry, tired, and dirty. Tariq prevented Emilio from committing the sin of theft by paying for the figs the boy was about to steal. He spoke in Maghrebi first, then in French, both times eliciting a dumb stare from the vagabond. Emilio said, "Italian," and Tariq was able to accommodate him. He offered Emilio lodgings on his floor. Emilio was ready to lose himself in the fragile sanctuary of the crowd. Tariq intoned the name of God and begged Emilio to stay. Emilio chose to go with him.

Heat and dust choked the glass-shop air. Tariq removed his fez and set it on top of a cracked display case. His bony forefinger signaled for Emilio to follow him into a confusion of wooden crates and boxes in the rear of the establishment. He pointed to a small space on the floor.

"You may sleep there. I'm afraid it isn't much, but it's better than sleeping on the street, or worse, in a jail cell."

Emilio thanked him, as his parents taught him to do when someone bestowed a kindness. When he asked Tariq why his face didn't repel him, the Moroccan said, "As you can see, I have one good eye. That means I can see only half what others see. I choose to see the half of your face that doesn't horrify."

Tariq left Emilio for a short time and returned with two glasses of steaming mint tea. He called Emilio over to sit and drink. Emilio climbed on a crate. His feet hovered inches above the floor. He sipped and upon tasting the hot drink slammed the glass down on the tray. Tea spilled over the rim of the glass and scalded his knuckles.

"Is it too hot?" Tariq asked.

"No, it's not that."

"What, then?"

Emilio described how he became a vagrant of the medina. When he spoke of Mr. Charles, Tariq looked pained, as if he wanted to atone for the wickedness.

"Yes, these things unfortunately happen in Tangier. Pray that Allah will soon deliver us from the vermin who infect our city with their perversions."

After tea, Tariq explained Emilio was welcome to remain as long as he liked. In return for food and lodging, Emilio would work around the shop. He handed the boy a broom. "You may start back here."

Such was Emilio's first day with Tariq.

•

The rain fell harder. Emilio didn't know how long he had been awake, nor did he know how long it had been raining or when daybreak would come. He closed his eyes, and the rain carried his thoughts homeward. He wondered if his parents were still searching for him or if they had given him up for dead. What of Serafino? Did he wander along the coastline awaiting Emilio so they could play? Or had he returned to the depths, convinced there no longer was an Emilio?

The rain ended as dawn approached. Emilio threw off the blanket. Had he been in his own home, he would have opened the shutters and drunk in the morning sea vapors. Here, there was no window. He took a few steps and uttered a cry. His large toe pulsated where the nail in a stray wood slat wounded him. He limped back to his mat.

"Good morning."

Tariq shuffled into the storeroom with breakfast. He noticed his new boarder was massaging his foot. He also saw droplets of blood scattered along the floor.

"You've hurt yourself."

"I stepped on a nail."

Tariq set the breakfast tray down and said, "I'll get you a bandage."

Emilio shook his head with disappointment at the sight of the food. It was the same breakfast he had eaten yesterday, couscous with honey and milk and a pot of tea. Emilio didn't like this food at all. It made his stomach feel heavy. Nonetheless, by time Tariq returned with the bandage, he was shoveling forkfuls of couscous into his mouth.

"You're a hungry boy. I trust you gave thanks for this meal?"

Emilio nodded a lie.

"That's good. You know that we owe everything to Allah's will. Now, let me see about your foot."

Tariq knelt at Emilio's side and wrapped the injured toe. He cast furtive glances at the pathetic face.

•

The noonday sun burned as if Tangier sat under a glass dome. Emilio swept the floor in the storeroom. He wore only a pair of shorts and slippers. Tariq watched him as he worked.

"Hello?" a voice called from the front of the shop in French. "Is there anybody here?"

"Let me tend to this customer, and then we'll eat," Tariq said.

The shopkeeper disappeared through the beaded curtain that separated the shop from the back room.

"Good day, sir, and how might I help you?"

The new voice had a familiar tone, contemptuous and refined. Emilio tiptoed across the floor and crouched three or four feet from the curtain.

There was Tariq in the middle of the shop floor, hands clasped, speaking like a shopkeeper determined to make a sale. The other participant in the conversation was Mr. Charles, a black patch over his left eye.

Emilio stepped back from the curtain. Did Mr. Charles know he was on the premises? If only he could hear what was transpiring in the other room, not that it would have made a difference, as Tariq and Mr. Charles were conversing in French. Emilio hid behind a crate and waited. The eternity that passed lasted a mere ten minutes.

"Emilio, where are you?"

That was Tariq. Emilio slid his face from behind the crate. Tariq was alone. The old man saw the uncombed hair and the dark crust with its thorns and serrated jaw line.

"What are you doing behind there? Come out here right now."

Emilio crept out from his hiding place. There was icy dread in his eyes.

"Emilio, why do you look so frightened?"

"It's that man you were talking to. What did he want?"

"He wanted to buy some crystal. Why is he important?"

"He was Mr. Charles."

"Indeed, indeed."

"Will he be coming back here?"

"He said he'd be back after lunch."

"O God, O God." Emilio paced back and forth. Tariq gripped him by the shoulders.

"Enough!" Tariq said. "Sit."

Emilio dropped to the carpet, drew his legs in, and rested his chin on his knees.

"If he finds me, he'll kill me."

"He won't find you, that is, if you stay back here and keep quiet."

"He's coming back after lunch. You said so."

"As I said, stay where you are and be quiet. Your Mr. Charles is a customer. He'll have no business back here."

Mr. Charles didn't return that afternoon, but it was no guarantee he wouldn't visit the shop tomorrow or the day after. Emilio's sleep that night was a tuneless symphony of nightmares haunted by the Englishman's voice.

To Emilio's relief, Mr. Charles failed to show up the next day. Still, Emilio was sure Mr. Charles would return. He was afraid to enter the selling area, because at that moment, Mr. Charles might walk into the store. He trembled whenever he heard Tariq speaking, because it could well have been Mr. Charles at the other end of the discussion.

Emilio's quarters were spotless, since he didn't have much else to do all day except sweep and tidy. When he wasn't cleaning the floor, he was rearranging the boxes or sleeping. A week passed, and Mr. Charles hadn't returned. Emilio felt a sensation of peace. He leaned on his broom and rested his cheek against the handle to relish the few calm moments that favored him.

"Emilio?"

He jumped. He didn't hear Tariq come in.

"Would you like to leave the shop for an evening? I've been invited to dinner at my cousin's house. He has extended the invitation to you, as well."

The cousin, whose name was Mustafa, lived on the other side of the medina. Like Emilio's benefactor, Cousin Mustafa was a widower bereft of the legacy of children. He was older than Tariq. He seldom left the confines of his cramped apartment and over the years settled into the static life of the recluse.

"I don't know," Emilio said.

"Emilio, you can't spend the rest of your life in this room. When was the last time you breathed fresh air?"

"I don't mind being here."

"Emilio, I won't force you to go. However, my cousin will feel slighted if you decline."

"What about Mr. Charles?"

"Do you honestly believe he'll be prowling the streets at night looking for you?"

"What about my face?"

"I've informed my cousin as to your condition, not that it's anything to be concerned about. He can barely see his own hand in front of his face. Now, has what I've told you alleviated your anxiety? If not, feel free to stay where you are."

Emilio worried about leaving the sanctuary of the shop for the uncertainty of the street. He also was afraid of offending Tariq. The shopkeeper was his savior, an old angel in an old fez. Tariq was so good and nurturing, like a grandfather. It would be discourteous of him to refuse.

Tariq told Emilio that Mustafa wasn't long for this world. Tariq made it a point to visit his ailing relative at least twice a week. He hoped Emilio would "illuminate my cousin's house with the sunshine of youth, because two old men sitting around and exchanging complaints make for a very depressing evening."

Emilio said yes.

"Wonderful," Tariq said. "My cousin is sure to be delighted with you, Emilio. We'll leave at nine o'clock. My cousin, strangely enough, dines late."

"What does he do with himself all day?" Emilio asked.

"He reflects on the years that have passed, mostly. He's a wonderful musician. After dinner, he'll play the oud. Wait till you hear him. You'll think his fingers are miraculous."

Tangier by night was as dark as a crypt. Shadows

stained the walls with odd geometric shapes. Pedestrians were silhouettes, their identifying features absorbed by the darkness.

For the first time in days, Emilio stepped into the open air. A woolen djellaba that was too large housed his body. It trailed behind him like a trawler's wake. Emilio kept one hand on Tariq's elbow. He refused to lift his head, feeling that with his eyes lowered, he was separated from all that transpired about him. If he refused to acknowledge the medina, then perhaps the medina would reciprocate.

He had no idea where Tariq was leading him. The streets all looked the same, stretching and snaking like the tentacles of a mythical squid. Scatterings of melody permeated the air, issuing from unknown instruments.

"How far is your cousin's house?"

"Not far."

"What time is it?"

"We won't be late."

"How old is your cousin?"

"It's impolite to ask about the age of an elder."

"I'm sorry."

They turned another corner and entered a courtyard. Emilio heard the low beating of a drum, but it was only his pulse shuttling through his head. He looked around at the windows, some closed and dark, others open and glowing with dull amber light.

"Does your cousin live in one of these houses?"

Tariq pointed. "He's in that one."

As they arrived, Emilio regretted his having agreed to dine with Tariq and Mustafa. He hated the djellaba. He predicted Mustafa would feed him the same food he ate at Tariq's. The dinner conversation would fly about him like a moth that evades capture: two men talking in a language he didn't speak. He wished he had stayed at the shop.

"Why don't you knock?" Tariq said when they reached the door.

Emilio rapped three times. Emilio looked at Tariq, whose gaze was set ahead.

"He's taking a long time to come to the door," Emilio said.

"It's what happens when age triumphs over the body."

Emilio heard the scuffling of feet within the house. The door opened, revealing a dim interior. Tariq extended his arm, bidding Emilio first entrance. Emilio mentally rehearsed the Maghrebi greeting Tariq taught him. As soon as he walked in, the door shut behind him.

"Good evening," said a voice to Emilio's right, but in Italian, not Maghrebi.

Emilio turned with a broad smile beneath his hood and then gasped in the agony of betrayal. Before him stood Mr. Charles, grinding his teeth, his arms folded over his chest.

Emilio realized to his horror there were only the two of them.

Tariq was gone.

THIRTEEN

Giulietta sorted through her clothes and discarded anything with color. These she either threw out or offered to her sister, who refused them.

"Emilio is not dead," Dona said.

"Then bring him to me."

Her life, it dawned on Giulietta, was a catalogue of deaths. It was a bequest from her late mother, whose function in life seemed to revolve around providing the gravediggers with a source of income. The woman bore five children, only two of whom survived to create their own families.

Giulietta's sister made her food, which she didn't eat. Her husband brought her coffee, which she didn't drink. They spoke to her, but she didn't reply. Wherever her eyes fell, she saw her son. When she finally did speak, one night before she and her husband went to bed, it was only to say, "I'd like to be where Emilio is." They were her last words on earth.

A week later on his boat, Leonardo cracked his skull when he tripped over a coil of rope and fell. He joined his wife in heaven.

FOURTEEN

Emilio cried on the sofa, doubled over because Mr. Charles had punched him in the stomach.

"If your performance as Madama Butterfly is intended to play on my sympathy, you're wasting your aria," Mr. Charles said. "I feel sympathy for no one, so you can caterwaul to the other side of the world as far as I'm concerned."

Mr. Charles's right hand clenched a riding crop. "I know what you're thinking, Emilio Giovanni Canto. It's written all over your face, or at least half your face. How could that nice old shopkeeper do this to you? One thing I've learned in my lifetime is that everybody has his price, especially in this hell-pit of a city."

His white makeup gave Mr. Charles the appearance of a circus clown.

"There's an American gentleman residing here—and I'm being frivolous in calling him a gentleman—who might take a fancy to you. I'll mention you when I see him next, assuming he isn't preoccupied laying his veins to waste."

Mr. Charles checked his watch. "My goodness, look at the time, and I haven't eaten yet. Emilio Giovanni Canto, you ought to be ashamed of yourself, keeping me from my dinner. Youth is so inconsiderate these days. I suppose you haven't eaten yet, either. I'll have Hassan bring you something, though Lord knows you don't deserve it after what you did to me. My thoughtfulness will do me in one day, I'm sure of it. I do have to say, though, the eye patch does give me a certain allure, don't you think? A je ne sais quoi, as the French say."

Mr. Charles opened the door a quarter of the way and turned back to Emilio.

"Will you remove your trousers please?"

Emilio just stared at him.

"Did you not hear me? I politely asked you to remove your trousers. Now, please do it before I'm forced to become disagreeable."

Emilio stood up and, with his back to Mr. Charles, unbuttoned his pants. He looked at the wall, his eyes following a crack that ended at the ceiling. He watched a small lizard creeping along the windowsill. He tried to concentrate on anything other than what his traitor hands were doing. The trousers fell around his ankles.

"Do turn around," Mr. Charles ordered.

Emilio knew it was pointless to disobey. He cupped his hands below his navel.

"I want you to give me your clothes. It's an insurance

policy against another escape attempt, not that you have a chance of getting out of here a second time. However, should the pipe dream cross your mind, Emilio Giovanni Canto, I don't think you'd want to consider running through the streets in your natural state."

Mr. Charles extended his arm. Emilio stepped out of his pants and bent down to pick them up with one hand, the other hand still serving as a fig leaf. He held them out to the Englishman.

"No, you bring them to me."

Mr. Charles flung the trousers over his shoulder.

"Do get acquainted with this room. You'll be here for a long time, that is to say, for the rest of your life."

As Emilio turned around to go back to the sofa, Mr. Charles's riding crop struck his buttocks.

"By the way," Mr. Charles said, "I was only being droll when I said this eye patch was appealing. I really don't like it at all, not a bit. I shall not forget it, you know. I don't care how much you beg me, you saucy rascal, I'll not forgive you. Emilio Giovanni Canto will pay for it. Yes, indeed, he most assuredly will pay."

Mr. Charles left, and Emilio heard the lock click, a sound so slight, yet with the foreboding of a cell door clanging shut. Emilio dropped onto the sofa and only then felt the sting of Mr. Charles's riding crop. He rubbed his backside. There was an unmade bed at the other side of the room. Emilio chose to avoid it, because he imagined the infamies that took place between its sheets. He looked through the open window, which brought soothing visions of the North African sky. The window was a seductress. He heard it encouraging him to pass through it once and for all, to find permanent relief on the courtyard cobblestones.

How long had it been since the regrettable morning when he stepped aboard the boat of that damned, drunken Portuguese? Was Rodrigo far from Tangier by now and reveling in his perfect deception? Emilio wanted to pray for deliverance, but to whom would he pray? God was dead to him or he was dead to God. He had forsaken his home and family in search of peace, only to learn there was no peace. It died the moment he said goodbye.

FIFTEEN

A head with searching eyes stared from the water at the beehive city and wondered where the object of its quest might be.

SIXTEEN

Orange spots coated the bottom of the white bathtub like a skin disease. Black ants crawled around the drain. Emilio turned on the water and watched the bugs float like dirt on the rising tide. He picked out the drowned insects and immersed himself in the lukewarm water. He wrapped a towel around his middle when he finished.

"Bath time, is it? I hope you used plenty of soap. You smelled a bit sour, if you want to know the truth."

Once again he faced Mr. Charles, who this time wasn't alone. Behind him, peering over the Englishman's shoulder, was another man, who was even skinnier than Emilio. His withered flesh was gray and hung from his bones like dead moss. It was hard to tell his age, he was so emaciated. He could have been forty, seventy, or anywhere between the two. Wire-frame glasses, the kind worn by grandfathers and bishops, balanced on his turtle-beak nose.

"Emilio Giovanni Canto," Mr. Charles said, "I'd like you to meet Mr. Moore."

Neither Emilio nor Moore spoke. Mr. Charles shifted his eyes from one to the other.

"No one has said hello," Mr. Charles said. "I'm beginning to question my talent as a host."

"Hello, Emilio," Moore said. He had the voice of a sick man.

Mr. Charles glowered. "Say hello, freak."

"Hello."

"Well, what do you think?" Mr. Charles inquired.

"He'll do," Moore droned.

"Did I lie about this face?" Mr. Charles asked, lifting Emilio's chin with the tips of his manicured fingers. Emilio gagged on the man's perfume. "Please tell me, did I lie?"

"No."

Emilio left the bathroom, followed by the men. He saw a pair of pressed trousers and a white linen shirt spread out on the bed.

"Put those clothes on," Mr. Charles ordered. "Mr. Moore will take you to his room. By the way, he paid for the clothes, so show a modicum of gratitude. I don't have to be explicit, do I?"

Emilio had no privacy while he dressed. The soft cloth was soothing to his skin. The pants were too long, so he had to roll up the legs. He buttoned the shirt all the way to his neck. The aroma of starch mingled with the soapy fragrance of his body.

"My, my, my, doesn't Emilio Giovanni Canto look

handsome! Moore, I can't tell you how much I envy you."

Mr. Charles looked ravenous. Moore looked bored. He picked at a black scab on the back of his left hand. Purple and brown blotches spangled both of his hands, as if a rare virus were devouring his body. He extended one to Emilio, who recoiled. Mr. Charles clutched his prisoner by the hair and pulled him closer.

"I thought I told you to show some gratitude," he growled. "Are you obstinate, or are you just plain stupid?"

Emilio took Moore's hand. It was cold and moist, like a frog's belly. Emilio tried to pull his own hand away, but Moore was strong for so dissipated a man.

"Don't worry," Moore said. "I'm not going to hurt you."

"See, Emilio Giovanni Canto," Mr. Charles said, "you have a new friend. Mr. Moore is such a nice man, don't you think? He buys you new clothes and wants to play with you. I wish I had someone like him to be my friend."

Moore slipped a skeletal arm around Emilio's waist. Emilio wanted to shake it off and knew what the consequences would be if he did. Moore pushed him forward. Mr. Charles opened the door. Emilio walked out, followed by Moore, whose fingernails bit him like a scorpion's pincers.

•

An unhealthy odor of sores and sulfur fermented the air of Moore's room. One of the shutters, broken off its hinges, lay like a toppled headstone below the window, leaving the room prey to the night's winged beings. Holes riddled the wall opposite the bed. It wasn't until Emilio moved further into the room that he saw the shotgun on the floor under a writing table. Yellowed newspaper pages lay across the floor and bedspread like stray palm fronds after a tropical storm.

"Why do you have so many papers?" Emilio asked.

"I don't like to throw anything out."

Moore pushed aside some of the papers and sat on the bed. Emilio hurried to the window, because it helped him commune with the world outside. He banged his foot against the fallen shutter.

"It's been broken for months," Moore said.

"Why don't you fix it?"

"I don't mind the mosquitoes. They have to eat, too."

Moore grabbed a cigarette case from the nightstand. He opened it and offered its contents to Emilio.

"Care for a smoke? They're real cigarettes."

"No, thank you."

"You don't want one, or you don't smoke?"

"I don't smoke."

Moore slipped a cigarette between his mummified lips. He stretched out on the bed, one hand behind his head. The cigarette dropped its ashes onto his shirt. He brushed them away every so often. He crossed and uncrossed his legs at the shins and took no further notice of Emilio.

When the cigarette burned down to his fingers, he dropped it in a dirty coffee cup on the night table. It hissed when it met the wet dregs at the bottom. Moore threw his legs over the side of the bed and sat up. He buttoned the top of his shirt and knotted his tie. Then he stood and walked over to the mirror on the bureau. He combed his thin red hair and rubbed pungent cologne on his face. He stared at his reflection.

"You know," Moore said, "I used to think I was as

hideous as sin. My head looks like it was yanked off a skeleton and attached to a live body. Then I saw you and decided I'd met my match. Are there any others like you wherever you're from?'

"No."

"Sui generis, eh? That's Latin. It means 'of its own kind.'"

Moore went back to the bed. He opened a bottle of whiskey and poured himself a half glass.

"Would you like a drink?"

"No."

"*Salud.*" Moore drank it down at once. He set the glass on the table and wiped his lips with his fingers. He pressed his hand against his chest.

"That hurt," he said. "I guess I'm getting old. I used to be able to drink three-quarters of a bottle and still shoot the wings off a seagull. Now, it just makes me sick. And still I drink. It's strange, don't you think so?"

Moore patted the bedspread and asked Emilio to sit next to him. The boy didn't move. Moore nodded. "Yes, I know," he said. "There's a stool behind you. Feel free to use it, if you like."

It was a three-legged footstool. Emilio positioned himself on it and sat hunched over.

"Can't you sit up any straighter?" Moore asked. "I know it's hard. At least try."

Emilio straightened his back and fell over on the floor. The stool landed on its side. Moore held his stomach and crowed.

"Forgive me. Are you all right?"

"Yes," Emilio said as he got to his feet. He righted the stool and sat down again.

"You're welcome to the chair by the desk." He pointed to a battered roll-top across from the bed. Emilio shook his head.

"Don't worry so much about sitting so close to me. I don't bite, at least not lately. I have bad teeth. Speaking of which, are you hungry?"

"Yes."

"Well, then, let's see how we can remedy the situation."

Moore passed Emilio to get to the wardrobe. He raked his fingers through the boy's hair. To Emilio's surprise, the touch seemed benign, almost paternal. Moore reached both hands to the top shelf of the wardrobe and brought down a blue tin canister trimmed with pink and white flowers. He carried the tin to the bed and, setting it down, pulled off the lid. He stuck his hand in and withdrew a small brown crock and a butter knife. He set them on the night table. His hand returned to the depths of the tin and this time came up with two flat biscuits. He opened the crock and spread dark purple jam on both cookies. Moore bit into one biscuit and offered the other to Emilio, who declined.

"I thought you were hungry."

"I'm all right."

"It's good. They're English digestives with black-currant preserve. Have one."

"No, thank you."

Moore chewed with a great deal of noise. Crumbs tumbled down his chin and onto the bedclothes.

"There's nothing wrong with it. Look, I'm eating it."

Moore continued to nibble and thought for a few silent moments. His mind lighted on Mr. Charles's account of the boy's ill-starred arrival.

"Oh, I see. This is plain jam, sorry to say."

Emilio just sat there, wondering and waiting. Why was Moore taking his time, drinking, eating, and smoking? And why was he being so friendly? He was nothing like Mr. Charles.

Moore ate Emilio's biscuit and washed it down with something clear he poured from a pitcher. He held the glass out to Emilio, who didn't take it.

"It's only water. I never mix my booze. It turns my stomach into a furnace."

He gulped down another glass, drank more whiskey, and then was back at the wardrobe. He brought out an oblong can. There was strange writing on its white label. Moore opened the middle drawer of the nightstand and took out a can opener.

"You'll like this," he said. "It's pâté from France."

The pâté coasted out of its case, as pink as flesh and mottled with black truffles. Moore cut several slices, laid one on a biscuit and gave it to Emilio.

"You have to believe it's all right. It came out of a can, for God's sake."

Emilio smelled the liver and licked it. He noticed that Moore treated the pâté as if it were a rare, precious object, taking small bites and rolling it on his tongue. He tried to do the same, but ate it in two greedy bites.

"My dear boy, you don't eat pâté like that. You really are famished, aren't you? What did that pompous old queen feed you?"

Moore handed him a larger portion.

"How old are you?" Moore asked.

"Fifteen," Emilio said between bites.

"Can you guess how old I am?"

"No."

"Guess."

"I don't know."

"I'm forty-eight."

Moore saw the doubt on Emilio's face and said, "Really, I'm forty-eight. I'm not lying. I look a lot older, I know. Every time I look in the mirror I seem to find a new wrinkle or new sag. I lost most of my hair ten years ago. Of course, all the junk over the years didn't help the situation."

Moore got up when he heard the faint knock. Mr. Charles's head, with its redundancy of chins, appeared when Moore cracked open the door. Emilio stiffened at the sight of him. Moore frowned.

"What is it, Ellsworth?"

"I apologize for intruding. I know it's incredibly rude of me. I was wondering how the two of you were getting on."

"We're fine, we're fine," Moore groaned.

"Emilio Giovanni Canto, are you being a good boy?" Mr. Charles asked.

"He's good," Moore assured him.

"I'm so very pleased to hear it. There's someone else who wants to meet our young oddity, so don't be too rough on him, Moore."

"You can have him back tomorrow," Moore said. "Now, if you'll excuse us."

He closed the door in Mr. Charles's face before the Englishman had the opportunity to bid them goodnight. Moore lay on the bed and reached for the bottle.

"You still hungry?"

Apologetic, Emilio said he wanted a slice of pâté. Moore obliged.

"I have to tell you," Moore said, "I've never seen anything like it before, your face, I mean. It really is quite extraordinary. I'm amazed you were able to make it this far."

Emilio's lower back was sore from sitting so long on the stool. He stretched and lost his balance again. Moore kept on talking. He pulled open the night-table drawer and took out, one by one, a book, then another, and then a third.

"Can you read?"

"Yes," Emilio said.

"These are all in English. I bought them from one of the booksellers in Tangier. They acquire them from stranded Europeans who are desperate for money. Those types are legion here. In any event, I have Milton, Jane Austen, and Virgil. Do those names mean anything to you? I suppose they don't."

"I know who Virgil is."

"Yes, on second thought, I imagine you do."

Emilio found it peculiar. All the man wanted to do so far was talk. He bought Emilio clothes and fed him tasty food. Moore no longer seemed so menacing. Emilio's fear began to melt away.

"Mr. Charles told me you're from America." Emilio said the country's name as if it were a synonym for "heaven."

"Yes, I was born in the United States, in Kansas, to be specific. I haven't been to the States in fifteen years."

"How come you left?"

"I had my reasons."

"What were they?"

"You're an inquisitive chap, aren't you? If you must know, I killed my mother. Shot her. Don't look so distressed. It wasn't intentional, I assure you."

"How long have you been living here?"

"Off and on, five years. I lived in Rome, which is where I met Ellsworth. I made brief stops in Indonesia, Spain, and England. I'm not fond of the English, you know. They have no respect for food. It's all bacon grease and pie crust. I despise this place, as a matter of fact, but it's easy to live here. Nobody gives a damn about anyone, so you're free to do as you please."

Emilio wondered about Moore's account. A man like him wouldn't kill someone in error, not even a parent. He glanced at the locked door. He was sure Mr. Charles was on the other side, listening. He imagined the Englishman disappointed by all the casual talk.

"Could I have something else to eat?" Emilio asked.

Moore sliced off two thick pieces of the pâté and gave them both to Emilio.

"Good, isn't it?"

Emilio nodded as he ate. Moore got up. A tender hand lighted on the boy's head. Emilio stopped eating. He sat there, his cheeks distended with half-chewed goose liver. This was the moment. Moore pressed his thumb into one of the barbs on Emilio's face.

"Those things are sharp, aren't they?"

He slipped his hands under Emilio's armpits and brought him to his feet.

"Relax. Don't be so nervous."

Moore returned to the wardrobe, leafed through his clothes, and wrenched a white blazer off the hanger. He slipped it on and left it unbuttoned. He stepped behind Emilio and rested his bony arrowhead chin on the boy's head. A shiver burrowed mole-like down Emilio's spine. His nostrils ached with the mothball vapor from Moore's jacket and the reek of sickness that wafted about the man. Moore asked, "Do you want to go out?"

Emilio's entire face was a question mark.

"Do you want to go out?" Moore repeated.

"You mean outside?"

"Yes."

Moore couldn't have been serious. This was only his cunning way of torturing Emilio. Moore knew that Mr. Charles intended to keep Emilio incarcerated. It was a heartless game. Emilio would say yes, and Moore would reply with a cruel grin, "I'm sorry. It's not allowed."

"Do you want to go out or not?" Moore asked. This time he sounded impatient.

"I can't. He won't let me out."

"Ellsworth?"

"Yes."

"He won't stop you if you're with me."

"You mean you'll really take me outside?" Emilio was hopeful.

"That's what I mean."

"Will he be with us?"

"Ellsworth? He never leaves the house at night. Besides, he and I never socialize. I'm not too fond of the man. Frankly, I detest him."

"Why do you live here?"

"I like the cheap rooms and the cheap dates."

Emilio made his plan. As soon as he stepped outside, he would run with all his might. Moore was too frail to chase him down. Emilio would find sanctuary where no one would ever be able to reach him. He would fend for himself. Never again would he be foolish enough to fall for the fraudulent benevolence of others. He would sleep only when fatigue overcame him.

"This is the last time I'm going to ask you, young fellow. Do you want to go outside, or would you rather stay here and suffocate?"

"I want to go outside."

"Very well, then. Let's get a move on."

Out in the hallway, Emilio heard unappealing human sounds coming from behind closed doors. Mr. Charles met them at the end of the corridor. In his teeth was the ubiquitous cigarette holder. "Now, don't you two make a lovely couple? I'm going to assume, my dear Moore, you've had a change of heart about a night with Emilio Giovanni Canto, and you're returning him to my custody. So be it. Please don't ask for a refund. I've banished the word from my vocabulary."

"No, we're going for a walk."

"You're taking a tour of the premises? That might be most enlightening for our new boy. We're having a busy night, you see."

"We're going out," Moore said.

"Out where?"

"Outside."

"You're joking, Moore."

"I never joke," Moore replied in a dry monotone.

"I'm most terribly sorry. I can't allow it."

"You always let the boys out with their customers."

"Not this one, I don't," Mr. Charles said, pointing to his eye patch. "He got away from me once. I'll be damned if I'm going to let it happen again."

"You're already damned, Ellsworth. He won't get away from me." Moore patted his breast pocket.

I will get away, Emilio thought.

"I can't risk it," Mr. Charles said.

"You don't trust me."

"Frankly, I don't. Nor do I trust him."

"Ellsworth, I'm in the mood for a stroll, and I want to take my companion with me. I paid you good money for him. I insist on it."

Moore tapped his breast pocket again. Mr. Charles exhaled a cloud of smoke that signaled fearful acquiescence. He was aware of the state of the walls in Moore's room. Between the drugs and the gun, Mr. Charles was sure Moore would one day assassinate him in his sleep. For this reason, there were four locks on his bedroom door.

"Keep him under your nose one hundred percent of the time," Mr. Charles said, forcing an imperious air in front of Emilio.

"Good night, Ellsworth." Moore's salamander eyes scowled at Mr. Charles. The latter looked away.

"Have a good evening."

Mr. Charles watched them descend the steps to the first floor. He listened for the door.

"Worthless junkie," he said under his breath. "That boy had better be back here tonight."

•

Emilio again was donning a djellaba, the same kind he wore the evening Tariq delivered him into the hands of iniquity. He saw old men who reminded him of Tariq, and he hoped every last one of them would fall and break a bone, suffer a heart attack, or lose a relative.

Emilio had planned to dash away as soon as he reached the streets, but he lost his nerve when he saw Moore touch his breast pocket in the hallway. Moore took him to a café. They sat at an outdoor table, Moore drinking mint tea and eating French tarts, Emilio having nothing. Moore slouched, sipping his tea and admiring the young Spanish and Moroccan men who passed by. He smoked a few cigarettes and ordered olives and bread. Every five minutes or so, the waiter came by with a fresh glass of tea. Emilio, who couldn't keep his eyes off the olives, began picking them off the plate one by one. An untouched glass of tea cooled before him. After the last olive, he started on the bread, ripping chunks from the loaf and slathering them with butter. Somewhere around them, somebody picked an indolent tune on a stringed instrument.

"I hate that music," Moore said. "It never ceases. No matter what time of day or night you go out, you hear it. It's always around you, like stale air. Incidentally, I have to congratulate you for the job you did on Ellsworth's eye. Everybody else in the house was quaking in his slippers after your achievement. I was rolling around on my bed laughing my ass off. It was better than heroin."

Moore raised his glass. "In all seriousness, though, Ellsworth has it in for you."

"He told me. So did Hassan."

"The leper boy is a sad case. Ellsworth beat him mercilessly because of you."

"You saw it?"

"He never does anything like that in front of other people."

"How do you know he hit Hassan?" Emilio asked.

"I know what Ellsworth is like."

"I feel bad for Hassan."

"Hassan's lucky he has a roof over his head, no matter what goes on under that roof. If he were on the streets, he'd never last. He'd be another dead kid."

Moore drank the rest of his tea before continuing. "You know, there's another reason I've stayed in that house all this time. Ellsworth is petrified of me. That's incentive enough for me to live there. It gives me a renewed sense of purpose in life."

Moore snapped his fingers twice to get the waiter's attention. He made a writing motion with his hand. The waiter brought the bill. Moore scanned the tally and shook his head.

"They always make sure you can't read the check."

He tossed a few dirham banknotes on the table.

"Let's go for a walk."

Emilio stayed a few paces ahead of Moore. Men cloaked in the darkness of thresholds and corners watched with inimical eyes. They made Emilio nervous. Moore paid them no heed. He was a familiar presence in the medina. The locals referred to him as the American Ghost.

Moore didn't doubt he would celebrate the half-century mark in Tangier. He thought of leaving for the Far East or South America or settling in Paris or Milan and living some semblance of a civilized life. Yet he knew he would never leave. The will to redefine his life wasn't there. Whatever resolve Moore harbored at this point was in a syringe. He was a charcoal sketch of what once was a finished human being. His name wasn't even Moore.

Emilio heard a voice in his heart that urged him to throw off his robe and escape into the recesses of the medina. His legs refused to obey. He could outrun Moore; he had no misgivings about it, but in his jacket Moore carried the means of taking him down.

His interior voice commanded him to flee, saying, "Go on, get out of here, you're free." His entire body shivered. The voice was insistent now. "Run away. Leave." But it didn't sound like his voice. Was it Serafino calling to him, finally reaching him across the sea miles? It didn't sound like the dolphin's voice, either. It sounded old and tired, a voice without strength, one that wanted to shout, but couldn't. Emilio realized then that it came not from inside him, but from behind him.

"Listen to what I'm saying. Beat it."

It was Moore. Emilio turned around. Moore was only four or five feet away from him. Emilio's eyes veered from Moore's face to his jacket. Moore stood there like a phantom. He stepped up to Emilio. Even hunched over, he seemed tall.

"I'm not lying to you," Moore said. "You're free to go."

Emilio didn't budge. The overlarge hood of the djellaba drooped down the sides of his face. His stomach was in knots.

"What's the matter with you?" Moore asked. "I'm telling you to get the hell out of here."

"You'll shoot me."

"I'll shoot you? Where the hell did you get that idea?"

"You have a gun in your jacket."

"I do?"

Emilio touched the inside pocket of Moore's jacket. It contained the cigarette case and nothing else.

"See?" Moore said.

"Why did you let Mr. Charles think you had a gun?"

"That should be fairly obvious. I had to put his mind at ease. Otherwise, you'd never have gotten out of there tonight."

Emilio bit his lower lip. "You're letting me go?"

"You catch on quickly, don't you?"

Unconquerable suspicions still had Emilio in their grip. "Why are you being so nice?"

The inquiry caught Moore off guard. No one had ever asked him that.

"Well, I ..." he stammered and then spoke with determination. "It's not so much that I'm being nice to you. It's that I'm not being so very nice to our Mr. Charles. Listen to me. You have a choice. You can go your way and live your life, such as it is, or you can come back with me and spend the night in my bed, because I paid for you, so I might as well get my money's worth. And once the night's over, you'll go back to Ellsworth, and I promise you, that overstuffed fairy will kill you one day. I saw it in his eyes, or I should say, eye. This is the last time I'm going to say it. Go away. Get the hell out of here."

Emilio ran down streets that were identical. He didn't dare look back. Emilio had no idea where he was going, but he knew he couldn't stop for a second. He could have asked Moore to show him the way to the dockside, where he might find a boat that would take him home. Or there he might find another like Rodrigo or Tariq or Mr. Charles. Or he might dive into the harbor and allow himself to drown.

Salvation did, in fact, lie at the end of his escape, although there was no way he could know it yet. It swam in circles, issuing cries that he alone would hear if only he were within listening distance. For now, he followed a bewildering network of passages that had neither beginning nor end nor led in any perceivable direction. He heard dark laughter coming out of doorways and voices without visible bodies calling after him in Maghrebi.

He fell against a stucco wall on a narrow street washed in the milk bath of the full moon. Emilio coughed and gasped for air. His sides ached.

Emilio began walking again, but with difficulty because of the pains that rode up and down his shins. The sea's odor was strong now, and as a seaside child, he was confident of his ability to pursue it. He reached the arch that was the gateway to the medina, and he passed through it with gratitude that he was able to accomplish this much.

He left the city and made his way to the beach, deserted and peaceful in the moonlit night. It reminded him so much of the beach outside his bedroom window that, for the first time in weeks, a feeling of safety graced him.

Emilio cast off the djellaba and his own hood and sat at the edge of the water, the sand as inviting as clean sheets. He lay back, thinking of everything and nothing, his thoughts as stirred as a shellfish stew, when a sweet voice called his name. He raised his eyes to the water and smiled, first in disbelief and then in joy in the knowledge that what he saw wasn't a hallucination.

"Serafino!"

•

Moore ignored Mr. Charles's foaming rage as he

probed his forearm for a useful vein. Boys in various stages of undress and their clients gathered outside the room.

"What the hell was going through that junk-addled brain of yours?" Mr. Charles screeched.

Moore couldn't find the vein. He rolled down his shirtsleeve and buttoned the cuff. Mr. Charles seethed.

"Are you listening to me?"

"Yes, mum."

"I knew I never should have let him out of the house. Damn it to hell, I knew it was a big mistake to trust you."

"Does this mean you want a divorce?"

"You think you're pretty funny, don't you?"

"I like to think so."

"I hate you, Moore. I swear to God, I hate you."

"That's not a very nice thing to say, Ellsworth."

Moore opened the night-table drawer and took out a clay pipe with a long, curved stem. He stuffed it full of cannabis that he kept in a mason jar. He held the pipe out to Mr. Charles.

"Here you go, Ellsworth. Have some. You could use it." Mr. Charles snatched the pipe and threw it across the room. It crashed against the wall and shattered.

"That was my favorite pipe," Moore said.

Mr. Charles bent over and plunged his face inches away from Moore's. "I'd like to strangle you with my bare hands, Moore."

"I've been sure of that for a long time, Ellsworth. It's a pity you don't have the guts to do it. Now, get that cake-batter face out of my face, or you'll need another eye patch."

On the other side of the door, overworked boys

agreed that somebody had to warn Hassan. But he already had hidden himself at the bottom of a wardrobe, his body curled tight as if in a burial jar. He trembled in his solitude, knowing Mr. Charles would find him. He closed his eyes and murmured verses from the Quran. As for Emilio, the poor leper hoped Mr. Charles would find him and drag him back. Hassan also hoped Mr. Charles would never find Emilio, because Mr. Charles would kill him, and no one in Tangier would know or care.

Mr. Charles paced like a pregnant lioness from one end of Moore's room to the other. He slammed his angry fists against his hips. "I'll find that skinny abomination. I did it before, and I'll do it again."

Mr. Charles grasped the doorknob. A sudden stinging sensation under his blowfish chin stopped him. He put his hand to his throat. He looked at the hand and his shirt. Mr. Charles bled and bled as if there would be no end to his bleeding. He turned to Moore, who stood before him waving the bloody razor like a conductor's baton. Mr. Charles's breath bubbled at the bottom of his violated throat. He clutched Moore's arms on his way to the floor, his one seeing eye aghast at the certainty of his coming demise.

"Don't look at me like that, Ellsworth. You should have known this was bound to happen."

Mr. Charles stopped breathing. Moore stooped over and placed two fingers on the man's pulse. He stood upright and kicked the dead, bloated body.

"That didn't take long."

Pondering the fresh corpse, Moore was curious. He lifted the eye patch and chuckled.

"Bravo, young fellow."

Moore picked up the bottle of whiskey and raised a toast to the late Ellsworth Charles.

"Maybe it's time to think about South America."

SEVENTEEN

Emilio found himself washed ashore. He lay on a deserted beach bordered a few hundred yards up from the waterline by palisades. He stared down the length of the shore. The land was barren, with neither trees nor shrubbery, only sand as white as flour. The sky, deep blue and regal, was empty, too, unmarred by sun, moon, or stars. None of this was familiar. Serafino hadn't brought him home.

Emilio stood up, took a faltering step, and stumbled. He looked down at his body and touched his chest and thighs.

"It's you, Emilio."

"Serafino! Where am I?"

"You're in the place I brought you."

"I can see that, but where is it? Why didn't you take

me home?"

"This is where I was told to bring you," the dolphin replied.

"Who told you to bring me here? Tell me."

Serafino didn't answer. His black eyes gleamed with the illumination of an inner light.

"Serafino, what's wrong with you? Please talk to me. I'm scared."

"I brought him, Mother," the dolphin said in the direction of the palisades.

Emilio looked toward the cliffs, then back at Serafino.

"Who are you talking to?"

Emilio's name issued from the rocks. It was a woman's voice, maternal and compassionate. He saw her and, of course, thought she was an illusion. Yet the more he stared, the more genuine she became. Believe what you see, she told him. She motioned for him to come. She was beautiful, so beautiful that her presence defined the word, and no word could ever define or describe what he saw. Clothed in veils and light, she looked as he always imagined she would on those many nights and mornings when he prayed for her intercession. When he reached her, Emilio fell to his knees and crossed himself. He, so unworthy and so hideous, was afraid to look at her. He closed his eyes. She told him to open them without fear. He wanted to speak, but what could he say to such an exalted one? She smiled, and the smile contained all the splendor of the universe. She laid her hands on Emilio's shoulders and commanded him to lift his head. She called her Son's name. Warmth unlike any that Emilio knew embraced him. One by one, the protrusions on the boy's unspeakable face broke off and fell on the ground.

EIGHTEEN

Federico tried many times to play fetch with Lucia, but the dog just sat when he threw the stick or the ball. She made him angry.

"Don't you know how to do anything? No wonder you and Crab Face got along."

Nor would the dog sleep at the foot of his bed. In fact, she didn't want to spend any part of the night in the house. Federico's father decided to keep her outside. One Sunday morning, as the sun was mounting the sky, Lucia began barking. The three of them—father, mother, and son—responded to her call and found her on guard, baying at the sea. Marco squinted through the early haze.

"What's out there, Papa?"

"It's only a dolphin."

Marco, Dona, and Federico went back inside to dress

for Mass. They had seen the dolphin, but they hadn't seen everything, for with the fabulous creature was Lucia's true master: Emilio, the ridiculed and reviled, now possessing a face made whole, a face luminous, immaculate, and yes, beautiful.

In his wide-open heart there was neither sorrow nor regret. Emilio knew joy.

www.ingramcontent.com/pod-product-compliance
Lightning Source LLC
Chambersburg PA
CBHW020628130626
46552CB00003B/1118